COME BY WATER

A RETELLING OF TAM LIN

TALES FROM KARNEESIA
BOOK TWO

CLAIRE TRELLA HILL

Come by Water

Cover Art by JV Arts

Paperback ISBN: 979-8-9883463-3-3

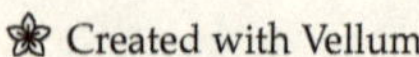 Created with Vellum

For all of us who have a fascination with water
And the more obscure fairy tales
But specifically Rosamund
For the Tricky Pixie version

'The night it is good Halloween,
When fairy folk will ride,
And they that wad their true-love win,
Miles Cross they maun bide.'

'But how shall I thee ken, Tamlane?
Or how shall I thee knaw,
Amang so many unearthly knights,
The like I never saw?'

— TAM LIN CHILD
BALLAD 391

ONE

The rain drummed incessantly against the windows of the castle keep for the fifth day in a row. It showed no signs of stopping, either, demolishing all Janet's hopes of escape from the circle of ladies and young misses that giggled and gossiped relentlessly.

Janet stabbed her needle violently into the handkerchief she was trying to embroider with a border of vines, narrowly missing her finger, and sighed.

After days cooped up indoors, they had run through all the tales fit for gently bred ladies, and now some of the younger girls had switched to local folk tales, myths, rumors, and what the villagers called haints. Janet hid an eye roll as Margaret wittered on, enjoying her audience.

"—And now they say that Carterhaugh is haunted!" Lady Margaret gushed, clutching her embroidery to her chest. All the other ladies in the sewing circle gasped with the horror of those with delicate sensibilities.

Janet ground her teeth.

The storm had most likely prompted the tale; they hadn't had a storm so long nor so wet in nearly seven years, the same time as the tragedy. With the nearly constant roil of war in Damaslar *somewhere,* it was only natural for such stories to crop up around abandoned or ruined homesteads, but Janet had a sore spot about Carterhaugh.

"Margaret," Janet finally said, cutting off the girl's long ramble about hellhounds with flaming eyes that prowled the property. "Do be quiet and stop spewing that bile. You know very well Carterhaugh is *not* haunted."

Margaret drew herself up straight, her pale face heating up. "How do you know? Sam Greenwald was passing that way just last week, and he saw something move in the mist! And if it wasn't a ghost, what was it?"

This time, Janet did roll her eyes. "Some tramp, of course, or someone hunting. But Carterhaugh isn't haunted."

"No one knows that for certain! When I think of what happened there, the family killed in that horrible fire and the boy drowned, why—"

"You won't malign the Lane family in my presence," Janet ground out, her dark eyes flashing. She made it quite clear she expected that to be the end of the matter.

Margaret pressed her lips together but said nothing. How could she? Janet was the daughter of the Earl of Anandale, and Margaret's father a mere baron. But all that afternoon, as the rain drummed the windows of her solar and the rest of the girls sewed in resentful silence, Janet couldn't get her mind off Carterhaugh.

She and the Lanes' son had been nearly the same age, and they had played together as children, getting into mischief and all manner of scrapes on the hills and dales between Carterhaugh and Anandale. They had been close, both only children, and spent as much time as they could together.

It wasn't all mischief. Sometimes they had wandered just for the sake of exploring, or fished in the river with their father's guardsmen, or helped Janet's mother with her garden. Nigh inseparable, they had been. She even recalled confidently declaring as a small child that she would marry Tam when they grew up. It felt as though her future always had Tam Lane in it.

Until the wars had come to their corner of Damaslar.

Janet stood abruptly, left her failed embroidery, and departed the solar to seek out her father. He was in his study, reading.

His gray hair shocked her, as it always did. He lived in her childhood memory as a tall and sturdy man with a head of bright blond hair. She wondered where the years had gone.

"Janet," he said, taking her brown hand, part of her mother's Cadruissi heritage. The earl had met and wooed Janet's mother when he had been very young and squiring for an older brother who had eventually died on the battlefield. When he had become the Earl of Anandale, her father had married her mother and brought her home to be Anandale's countess. She had been gone three years from the influenza.

Janet suspected that was what had turned his hair so gray.

Winding her braids around the fingers of her free hand, she asked, "Papa, what has become of Carterhaugh?" Her braids had come down from their pins again, and at this point in the afternoon, she gave up on putting them back.

"It's empty, abandoned." Her father shrugged, glancing at the map of the surrounding lands on the wall of his study. To the southeast of Anandale, Carterhaugh remained marked as a holding of the Lane family, even though all the Lanes were dead or gone.

"No one owns it?" Janet pressed.

"I don't suppose so. Why?"

The words came out before she could stop them. "I want it."

The earl raised an eyebrow.

"As... a dowry." Janet slid her eyes away, glancing out the window of the study into the drizzle outside. "It's good land, and...."

Her father squeezed her hand. "I know," he said quietly. "I miss them, too. You're not worried about it being haunted?"

"*Ugh*, spare me," she muttered.

He laughed. "All right. If you want Carterhaugh, it's yours."

She looked up in shock. She had been expecting a far longer battle.

He smiled. "You've asked for little enough for a dowry. Seven years is long enough for a holding to pass from one family to another. I'll send the necessary papers and money to the capital to be witnessed. It will be a part of your marriage settlement."

"Thank you, Papa," Janet said, and threw her arms around his neck.

He laughed and stood to hug her properly. "Does this mean you will make up your mind about all the suitors that come daily knocking on our door?"

Janet hid her look of disgust in his shoulder. "Perhaps."

THE SUITORS WERE NUISANCES. She was her father's only child, and a girl besides, so she *must* marry to secure the estate. And Anandale was a fine property, with plenty of fertile farmland and good, loyal tenants, and many lords wanted that to increase their holdings. Younger sons wanted the title that came with it. For those assets, it seemed, any number of men would put up with a headstrong and half-Cadruissi wife, and they had camped on Anandale's doorstep and filled their halls to prove it.

But she'd rather not marry someone that "put up" with her.

At the high table for supper, Janet stared into her wine glass and, not for the last time, cursed the laws that put estates into the hands of husbands. She was capable and smart; she knew she was —didn't she always assist Old Ivar with the accounts? Hadn't she helped the captain of the guards organize the keep and drill the soldiers when it looked as though a disagreement between neighbors on their border would explode into open warfare? It hadn't, but they had been prepared to defend their land, and had put away enough food to last a siege.

In Altesia, *they let women inherit and run their own land. They don't have to wait for a husband to take ownership of it.* She swirled the dark red vintage her mother had put down and sighed.

The new countess sniffed, her long nose and turned-down mouth indicating her disapproval. Janet reluctantly straightened.

The earl had remarried after Janet's mother died, a last-ditch effort to produce a male heir. Janet was his only child that had lived past her fifth birthday. The former Lady Insopha, now Countess Insopha, had had two sons by her previous husband before he died in battle, and seemed a likely choice. So, the earl had proposed marriage, and the woman had jumped at a better title, leaving the sons with her late husband's family. They had been married for a little over a year, and so far, Janet had seen no signs of success. That only made her stepmother more unbearable. The idea that Janet and her as-yet-undecided husband might inherit Anandale did not sit well with the countess.

Resisting the urge to prop her chin on her fist, Janet peered at the hopeful swains arranged on the lower tables. A few she could see herself tolerating—the ones that didn't boast of their prowess on horseback or beneath the sheets, ones who actually seemed to listen when she spoke. But the others, like Sir Noarvan and Sapher of Geran, with their wide smiles and lingering eyes as they assessed the riches of Anandale—absolutely not.

Her fingers tightened around the stem of her goblet as the servant cleared away the plates. Anandale was *her* land, rules of inheritance be hanged. Hers and no other's!

Though… now that she thought about it….

Janet's head came up.

Carterhaugh was hers now, too.

CHAPTER

TWO

As soon as the rains stopped, Janet rode south to Carterhaugh. The trees still held water, and she twitched irritably every time the wind shook the boughs and showered her with droplets. Her horse's hooves made little sound on the sodden ground.

She traveled by road for most of the way, even though the mud was a trial, in order to avoid any new lakes that the rain might have made. Only when she reached the fork at Miles Cross over the river did she cut across the fields and woods.

When the trees cleared, Janet dismounted and took in the ruins of Carterhaugh.

After the Lane family's deaths, the undefended land had been subject to numerous battles and destruction as passing armies had used it as a convenient battlefield. The earth still displayed the ravages of fighting. The recent rains filled the torn turf and uneven terrain with deceptive puddles of murky water under the low-hanging trees. The bend of the river, just visible in the distance, became a wide pool, swallowing up its banks, doing its best to turn the land into a bog. It felt as if the swampland to the south was encroaching on their territories.

Seven years ago, the house had burned with most of the Lane

family inside. Whether it had been an accident or someone had fired the house, no one knew.

Now the half-burned edifice loomed out of the gloomy mist. Though the rain had stopped, the sun still hid behind clouds.

In the gray light, Janet tied her horse to a branch and stepped into silence. No birds sang in Carterhaugh, no wind blew, no leaves rustled. Everything lay as still as—death.

I was a fool to come, she thought, as the cool air chilled her bare legs, her skirt still tucked up in her belt from riding. *There are no happy memories left here. Only ghosts and a ruined land.*

It had been more foolish of her to ask her father for the holding. What would she do with it? What worth did it have now? Even if there was virtue left in the soil, there were surely bodies lying underneath, just waiting to meet a plow's blade. And no one would come to work the land in such a forlorn, forgotten place. All the families who had lived here had moved on long ago, and any others would be gripped by the same horror and superstition from Margaret's tales.

Janet trailed through the mist, stepping around deep pools and mossy trees towards what had once been the gardens behind the hall. She found a hole in an overgrown hedge and stepped through.

Her breath caught in amazement. Mist and dew mingled in the air and twinkled silver on the leaves of the wild and thriving flowers. Honeysuckle grew in abundance, and petunias, and violets and marigolds and columbine mixed with touch-me-nots and jack-be-nimble, spilling out of what had once been orderly rows and flowerbeds to lie across the path in thick, wild tangles.

In the center of the garden, dark lily pads and pale white water lilies choked a sunken ornamental pond Janet distinctly remembered being pushed into once upon a time. If memory served, the water was very cold. If any of the goldfish still lived in the pond, they must not have seen the sun in many a year. Janet edged carefully around it as she moved through the garden; rain-fed as it was, it overflowed its banks.

And the roses! Janet's mouth hung open as she sidled around the lupine and lily of the valley. Roses in every shade imaginable grew tall and high—higher than her head in some places, climbing up rotting trestles and stone walls and convenient trees. Their heady scent hung in the air, as thick and sweet as treacle.

Some were the tiniest of buds, tightly closed, but others were in full bloom, stretching up to the light. The shadows hid the green, sharp thorns underneath the blooms, tangled as they were. Petals lay everywhere on the tall, uncut grass.

Janet bent her head and reached for a creamy pink rose, half open and tilted cunningly towards her with an iridescent bead of water perched upon the outermost petal. She inhaled the fragrant scent and closed her eyes, enchanted.

"Why have you come here?"

Janet gasped and whirled, her skirts slapping her bare legs. Her hand stung. She had broken off the rose and caught her hand on the thorns.

In front of her stood a young man, dressed in the same green as the garden, with pale skin and dark hair and beard. His green eyes fixed unblinkingly on her.

"Who are you?" she breathed, burying her wounded hand in her skirt. She had not heard him approach.

He did not answer her. "Why have you come to Carterhaugh?" His eyes bored into her, knowing and sharp.

"Why shouldn't I come?" Janet said, trying to control the shaking in her voice. "My father gave the land to me as a dowry. Why have *you* come here?"

"Those are my roses," the man said, the green of his eyes the bright fresh sap of a plant. "I did not give you leave to take one."

She was tempted to retort, *"Didn't you hear me? If Carterhaugh is mine, then the roses are mine, too."* But she suspected he'd take just as little notice of that as he did her previous words. There was something wrong with his eyes….

"So it is," she said, proffering the pink rose. "I didn't mean to break it, but you *did* startle me," she said reproachfully. "Where did you come from?"

He did not reach for the rose. "You must give me something for the rose."

No, I don't; it's mine! But it was probably best to humor the stranger alone with her in this garden. And just her luck, this was a freshly laundered gown, Janet thought, disgusted. No coin, nothing in the pockets. "I've got my belt," she gestured to the fine leather. "It's worth quite a bit."

He shook his head. "No." In all this time, he hadn't blinked.

"My cloak?" She reached for the clasp to the fur-trimmed cloak. It was mud-stained, but well-made and—

"No."

She didn't care for the direction this conversation was going. "My ring?" She held up her hand so he could see the jewel there.

"No."

She swallowed and pressed her lips into a thin line. "Then I'll give you my name," she said firmly. Something he could not refuse. "I am Lady Janet of Anandale, daughter of the Earl of Anandale."

The young man's eyes slowly closed. Opened. Blinked again. Something of the intense haze around him faded, and the third time he blinked, his eyes no longer shone the bright, sickly hue. They were a perfectly ordinary shade of brown.

"Janet?" he said in an altogether different voice, stepping towards her.

"Do you—know me?" she stammered, stepping back.

"Janet," he said warmly, the corners of his mouth turning up. "Still turning up where you shouldn't with mud on your hem." His eyes glanced down and then back up. "But a beauty all the same."

She blushed hotly as his gaze skimmed across her bare legs. Then his words sank in. "Mud on my—"

She met eyes that sparkled with mirth.

The hand that reached for hers was thin and translucent, like a sunbeam through cloud or the sparkle of a cobweb covered with dew. She could see the pattern of grass through the sleeve. But when he touched her cheek, the flesh was hard and cool against her skin, roughened with work and calluses from holding a sword.

"Who are you?" she whispered, her hand coming up of its own accord to grasp his where it cradled her face. Those eyes struck a chord in her and made her shake. "*What* are you—are you flesh, or spirit?"

"You know me, Janet," he whispered. "I am Tam Lane."

"Tam," she gasped. Her heart leapt within her, and when he pulled her to him, she went gladly.

JANET WOKE in the garden alone. Her cloak had been spread over her, and she lay in a nest of flattened grass. Silence reigned. No birds sang. Not even an insect chirped in the gray stillness of impending twilight.

She sat up. The garden looked just the same, except the light was gone. What was once full of life and beauty had transformed into a gray and dismal scene. And empty. Her heart caught in her throat. "Tam?" she called.

No answer.

Janet stood and shook out her skirts, pulled grass from her hair. "Tam?" she called again. Where had he gone?

She hunted through the garden for any sign of another person until the light faded from the sky, but she found nothing. No footprints in the mud, no branches snagged on clothing and snapped. Not even the impression of another body in the grass beside her. It was as if her spectre from the past had disappeared into thin air.

Did I imagine him? She wondered frantically. *Was he really there?*

Had it been Tam Lane at all?

She put a hand to her forehead, retracing the events of the garden, the nearly magical light and her overwhelming joy that her best friend in the world was alive again. That he had come back to her. And the firm conviction, as she had wrapped her arms around him, that every moment of sorrow she had suffered was now untrue.

Janet's heart sank and she covered her face. Ahead of her lay home and father and the suitors, and no escape. "You left me once, Tam Lane. Why did I think anything would change?" she whispered to her horse as she slowly rode away from Carterhaugh.

Over the last few months since riding to Carterhaugh, Janet had listened hard for any rumor of the Lane family and inquired about any strangers newly come to the area, any travelers that matched the description of the man she had seen in the garden of his childhood home. But she had not heard anything.

Questions pelted back and forth in her mind incessantly. Where had Tam been these past seven years? Where had he gone? Why had he disappeared when she needed him so?

And in moments of deep doubt, she wondered if she had been deceived by only seeing what she had so longed to see. Had she imagined the whole thing entirely?

She had no answers for her questions…except to the last.

Janet spread her hands over the front of her dress, where her stomach just barely curved. She would have been able to hide for much longer, to figure out what to do, if only her stupid maid hadn't run to the countess when the girl spied Janet throwing up every morning that week.

"You must confess, Janet," her stepmother said, whirling mid-stride from her path pacing up and down in front of the large fireplace in her rooms. "Who is the father?"

When Janet said nothing, the countess rounded on the earl who held his head in his hands. "You must force her to speak, husband. She must be married before word travels."

"No," Janet said firmly.

Her father and stepmother turned to look at her. "If you won't say, then pick one of your suitors and marry him as soon as may be," her stepmother said, sniffing. "Once you're married it won't matter who the babe's father is. If you do it early enough, your husband may even think it legitimate."

"No," Janet said louder. "I'll marry none of them."

"Aegland, speak to her!" the countess implored the earl. "No man will have her when she's ruined!"

Her father drew his hands over his beard that seemed to sprout more gray hairs overnight. Janet hated that she might be the cause. "What will you do, daughter mine?" he said sadly. "If this was none of your choosing, I'll bring the man to justice if you'll name him. But if you name him not...."

The words tasted like bile on her tongue, but she spoke them all the same. "No, Father. I'm to blame."

"Some peasant's get, then," her stepmother decided. "You've lowered yourself with a stable boy or tinker's son, like a common maid. Don't you know your duty, girl? What you owe your family?"

"I know what I owe my family," Janet forced through numb lips.

"But you'll neither marry to save your reputation nor name the man?" the countess demanded, her mouth tight and pinched.

And have you think me mad? Janet closed her eyes and shook her head.

The countess blew out her breath in a strong, exasperated gust. "Then you must get rid of it," she said briskly.

Janet's head shot up.

"My maid has knowledge of herbs, potions," the countess went on. "You will go with her to the herb gardens tomorrow and pick what's needed, and then the matter will be at an end."

"No." She closed her arms protectively about her waist.

"Either name the man, or pick the herbs," the countess said in a voice equally stony. "Choose."

JANET LEFT the empty basket beside the herb plot and walked to the ornamental fountain that marked the separation of the herb and vegetable gardens from the flower garden. She had sent the countess's maid away once the woman had pointed out all the herbs needed. But how far would her obfuscations and deflections take her? If the countess put her mind to it, she'd make the drink herself and pinch Janet's nose shut with her long, sharp fingernails as she force-fed it to her.

Tam Lane had been her closest childhood friend. They had climbed every tree for miles and had fallen out of at least half of them. No pie was safe from their fingers. No cat un-petted. She could still see that grin of his, when he came up with another fool idea. She hadn't known a beard could change a face that much.

She flushed and sat down on the lip of the fountain. It was a good beard, though. He had been a far cry from the gangly boy she remembered.

No one quite knew what had happened that terrible night at Carterhaugh, but all the bodies of the Lane family had been found —most had died from smoke, not the fire itself. All except Tam.

She had cried for days and days, picturing him cut to ribbons by bandits or carried away and pulled under by the river. Never once had she thought him alive.

But alive was…not quite the word for it. He had been here one moment and gone the next, ethereal. A haint? Fae-touched? But he couldn't be dead, Janet knew, pressing a hand to her stomach. The child couldn't be denied.

"Oh, Tam," she whispered, trailing her fingers through the fountain's water. "I don't know what to do."

A hand came out of the fountain and closed around her wrist.

Janet sucked in a breath to scream. Before it escaped, a head broke the surface of the water.

"Janet," Tam Lane said, water dripping from his face and beard as he knelt in the fountain beside her, looking for all the world as if she had pushed him in.

Janet said something decidedly unladylike. "You scared ten years off my *life*, Tam Lane!" Her heart still beat a mad tattoo in her ears, and she tried to rein in the thoughts that had scattered to the four winds when she saw him. "What in the name of the ten stars of Mar are you *doing in my fountain*?"

"You called me by water, so I came." He looked puzzled, his eyes flickering to green for a moment, but then they settled back to plain brown. He smiled at her. "Is all well with you, Janet?"

"Is all *well with me*?" she repeated, her throat tightening from the swell of conflicting emotions. "Not at all! Tam, where did you go? Where have you *been*? You left me alone!"

"I was...I was called away against my will. I'm sorry; I never meant to leave you," he said. "But I'm here now—"

"Three months later!"

He paled, beads of water dripping down his face. Again, his eyes flickered that strange green of freshly snapped rose stems she remembered from the garden, from before he recognized her. He shut his eyes and took a deep shuddering breath, and when he opened them again, the green had gone. "Has so much time passed?" he said hoarsely.

"How long did you think it had been?" she whispered.

"A week." He swallowed. "A long, interminable week. I haunted Carterhaugh every chance I could when her gaze was far from me, to see if I could find you again...." He clasped her hand. "Forgive me, Jan. I did not want to leave you. And *never* for so long, but...." His expression was shattered.

"You were called away," she repeated slowly. Her heart started to pound. "What called you away? Tam, what happened to you?" Janet gripped his hand tighter.

"I was taken by the Queen of the Bog."

Janet's mouth fell open, and her free hand came up to clutch at her throat. "Aelwa? She of the faefolk, whose house is Fensalir? But that's just a tale told around winter fires. They—they make them up!"

"They make up some of the stories, but she is real, and faefolk. That's where I've dwelt for seven years."

"But you're not *dead*; they say Aelwa holds court with those who sleep under the water and the peat. Tell me you're not dead," Janet begged.

He smiled at her sadly. "I'm not dead. Just—caught between." Then he frowned. "Though...I don't know *how* you could have called me."

"What do you mean?"

"That night—the night the house burned. My uncle pushed Mother down the stairs. They had been quarreling. He wanted money, always more money. He had bled us of funds for years. She wouldn't give him any more. She wouldn't waste my inheritance on him, she said. He pushed her, and she fell." He swallowed. "She broke her neck. I can remember calling her name, looking up the stairs at him standing there, with such a look on his face.... Then he started towards me. I ran out the door and into the forest."

Janet clutched his hand. "What about the fire?"

"Mother had been holding a lamp. I think the drapes caught. I should've...." He shook his head. "I think I was heading for Anandale, to get help, but I lost my way in the night, crazed and panicked as I was. I fell in the bog. Aelwa found me," Tam said. "She took me to her home in the peat, nursed me back to health. But then she wouldn't let me leave."

She pressed her hand to her mouth.

"I'm bound to Carterhaugh and Aelwa's waterways, but she promised I could always come when family called." His mouth twisted. "It was one of her tricks. I didn't know then that they had all died." He glanced around the garden. "But here I am. At Anandale. How is it possible?"

Janet swallowed the lump in her throat and stilled the tremble in her lips. She placed a hand on her stomach. "Tam. I have to tell you something."

His brown eyes flicked from her face to her hand. He stilled.

Janet bit her lip. "I—"

Tam surged further out of the fountain and kissed her, hard, his hands cradling her face. His beard scraped against her skin as her lips opened to him. "Janet," he whispered, pressing kisses her mouth. "Really?"

Janet nodded, tears pricking her eyes. She clutched him, uncaring of the water soaking her gown. She was afraid he would disappear again. Her heart wouldn't bear that.

"What's the matter?" he asked, spying her face. "Do—do you not want it?"

She hated the despair in his voice. "No," she shook her head, "I *do*. But my father and stepmother have found out, and she has said if I don't name the man or choose a suitor, I must get rid of it."

For a moment, Tam looked very fierce, a green flash in his eye as his jaw worked. Then he blinked, his face softening. "Your mother is dead, then? Ah, Jan, I'm sorry."

His quiet, kind voice and the childhood nickname made the years-old grief spring from her eyes again, and he held her tight as she cried.

"Will you come with me to my father?" Janet said after a time, after wiping her eyes on his tunic. "You can explain, help him understand—"

"Jan, I want to, more than anything. I would stand with you against any judgment, but I can't leave this fountain, and if you leave, I must go. It's only your call that keeps me here. I fear she will notice—" His face froze. "Three months, you said? It's—it's autumn?"

"Yes. Why?" Her throat tightened. "What's put that look on your face?"

"I'm sorry, Janet. If it's been three months, that means...."

"What?"

"It means my time is almost up." He tried to smile, even as tears glittered in his eyes. "Forgive me for leaving you again."

A rush of fierce fury rose up in her. "I'm *not* going to lose you again, Tam Lane. Tell me what hold she has on you. Tell me how I can help."

CHAPTER

FOUR

hree days later, in the dead of night, Janet crouched at Miles Cross where the road forked over the bridge of the Rhymer River.

It had been difficult to escape from the maids who dogged her every step on orders of her stepmother, but the castle had several exits that didn't exist on any map to allow the family to escape in the event of a siege. Her father had shown them to her years ago. It was just a matter of waiting until all the maids in her room were asleep before she snuck out. She had made her way to the river and held her gray cloak around her, waiting.

"All Hallows," Tam had said, after she had worn down all his protests and his worries. "It must be All Hallows' Eve, three days hence. The changing of the season. The boundaries between the living and the dead are weaker then, easier to cross. Then does Aelwa's court ride out to circle her demesne. You must wait at Miles Cross. You'll have the best chance."

"Chance for what?"

"To catch me." He looked grim. "Else I'll be part of Aelwa's teind to the bog."

The words had made her stomach sink. Aelwa was said to cast followers—or sometimes unfaithful lovers, or those who had profaned her name—into the bogs every seven years. The reasoning for this was just as varied, but whatever the goal, Janet's resolve hardened into iron.

"It's been seven years she's had me," Tam had said. "She needs a teind to replenish her magic. I think my time is up."

"Not if I say it isn't," Janet had declared, fierce as a tiger. "I'm not going to let her keep you or kill you. You're mine."

In the dark, blowing on her fingers for warmth, Janet listened to the rush of the river below her hiding spot, on the bank up near the bridge trestles. The water was still high from the rains, so it wasn't far to the river's edge. She had to be careful not to slip. Overhead, Janet heard the rumble of thunder. *Please*, she thought, *no more water.*

In the darkness, a faint green light flicked to life, dancing above the water. Janet squinted at the far-away glimmer in the darkness as it became two, then four, then eight, and soon the lights danced above the surface of the river, setting the landscape ablaze with fairy lights.

They've come by water, Janet realized, staring at the small dancing globes.

Slowly massaging life back into her legs, Janet watched the procession of the Dead Court. They came in twos and threes wreathed by the unearthly light, knights with strange faces holding standards and riding kelpies, the horses of the waves.

"I hate asking this of you," Tam had whispered. "I don't know what I'll do—what they'll make me do. I could hurt you, Jan."

"If you don't tell me," she had growled, "then I'll show up not knowing what I need to know, and make some blunder, and get us both caught, so you had better tell me, Tam Lane, and tell me now."

"Not the black steeds," Tam had said, "and not the brown, but the milk-white mare—that's how you'll know me. You must hold me fast, and fear me not, no matter what I do—no matter what you see—and only then will I be free. You mustn't let go, Jan."

"I won't fail," Janet had said then, and said again now seeing the coats of the fierce and somewhat serpentine kelpies change from black to brown. She stood in the shadows, and then had to steady herself. They were all still in the river. How would she get Tam out?

The brown kelpies processed under the bridge, and then came a kelpie as white as milk, with a knight dressed all in green on its back. The helm he wore obscured his face. The knight rode beside and slightly behind a blood-red kelpie, and on that steed sat Aelwa.

Janet had no doubts as to the woman's identity. Her face was wreathed by long, black hair hanging loose about her shoulders and tinted by the green wisps. A wreath of cranberries and purple pitchers crowned her brow. Her red lips curved up in a proud, haughty smile.

Janet's heart sank at the deadly beauty that the faefolk queen wielded. How could she oppose a force like that—who had power at her beck and call? Who could squash Janet like a bug?

Her hands clutched her waist. If Aelwa hurt the babe….

Janet's gaze narrowed on the queen's hand. Her fingers wrapped around the reins of the milk-white kelpie, leading Tam's horse like one would lead a child's, or a lamb to the slaughter. The queen didn't even trust him that much.

Maybe she knows, Janet thought. *Maybe she knows that, even if the chance to escape is slim enough, he'll take it.*

I am his chance. Her promise rang through her head, and she clenched her fists. *And I'll not fail.*

As the steeds swam even with her, Janet took a deep breath and ran, launching herself down the steep bank and through the air, tackling the knight off the white kelpie and into the river water. The river made the knight's movements sluggish and slow, but he struggled in her grasp even so. Janet's face broke the surface as he thrashed. She took another deep breath, not bothering with trying to swim. She had purposefully aimed low, and her arms were clenched tight around his ribs so he would be able to swim for the both of them.

Although leaving his arms free might have been a miscalculation.

Janet ducked her head under the water and just missed a mighty swing from a gauntleted fist. The water roiled with the knight's motion—and he was still in full armor.

Bloody Perrin and the ten stars of Mar, Janet thought, and then she could barely think anything at all.

The figure in her arms shivered and shifted, the armor falling away from the body. The flesh sprouted fur and fangs, not to mention talons. Janet barely missed the snap of the wolf's sharp teeth. She swallowed some of the river water as the animal desperately tried to get out of the river and shed the dead weight around its middle.

Don't let go, she reminded herself. *Don't let go.*

One particularly strong thrash brought her out of the water. She coughed mightily, managing to sneak another breath before she was under again.

"Hold me fast," his memory told her as what she held changed again. *"Fear me not."*

Now a frantic stag that paid no mind to the weight on his back swam desperately for the shore. When its hooves found purchase on the bank, Janet thought, *oh no,* right before they surged out of the river. The stag immediately began to plunge madly, throwing its head back to see if its antlers would connect. Coughing water, she dug her fingers into fur and muscle, ignoring the gashes in her arms that shot pain through her body.

Then the stag shrank, boiling down into something lithe and green and slippery—an adder that opened its mouth, ready to bite.

"Fear me not," Janet chanted through bloodless lips, clenching the smooth coils that tried to slide through her fingers, "fear me not—"

Right before the strike, the adder grew larger, shifted form—and became a man.

Janet opened her mouth, then stopped.

The man she held was blond and freckled, with sickly green eyes. He smiled at her with a sly, mocking grin, and said in an unfamiliar voice, "Little fool. You picked the wrong man, I'm afraid."

Her stomach sank, and a drop of water slipped off her nose. It wasn't him. She had chosen wrongly. It had never been him at all.

"He confessed all, and I volunteered to take his place. He likes our court well and does not want to leave. He was just having a little fun with you, lass." He tilted his head, shrugged idly. "He doesn't want you."

As her heart quailed, her grip faltered.

"*I love you, Janet,*" Tam had told her, holding her hands as he knelt in the fountain at Anandale. "I always have, since we were children and you tripped me into a mud puddle. If you'll have me, I'll marry you and gladly. I want the babe to have my name. I swear to you, Jan."

"I believe you," she had confessed. "And you've no idea how much I've missed you these past seven years."

"I want to come home to you, whether that's here or Carter-haugh, or anywhere. I love you."

"I love you, too," she had whispered. "And I won't let go. I promise."

Hold fast. Fear not.

Her eyes sharpened, even as tears squeezed through them. "Take your faefolk lies and shove it," she snarled, digging her nails into his ribs hard enough to break the skin, hard enough to bleed.

And as his blood fell to the earth, the illusion shivered, shifted —and burned away, leaving a pale and shaking Tam Lane in her arms. "My Jan," he whispered, touching her cheek. The hand was solid and real. She could not see through it.

"You're naked," she sniffed. "Can I let go now?"

He laughed, a sound she hadn't heard in seven long years.

They both sat up, and she peeled her sodden cloak off from its dead weight at her neck and gave it to him. It was none too warm soaked with river water but would serve as a covering for now. They helped each other to their feet, and only then realized that the procession still waited in the river.

Aelwa watched them both with dark, murky eyes as her kelpie champed at its bit. Her mouth had darkened so much it was almost black. "How did you do it?" she demanded, in a voice of wind through reeds by water. "How did you steal away my best knight, you shameless chit?"

Janet clutched Tam's hand in her own. "He was never yours," she said, lifting her chin. "He was mine long before you stole him away. I took him back."

"Family," Tam said. "You said the key to my freedom lay with family."

The queen looked between them, realization growing in her eyes. She bared her teeth, sharp as knives and none so clean. The purple pitchers of her crown moved restlessly, the carnivorous plants searching for prey.

"You are bound," Tam said tightly, only the strength of his grip around Janet's hand belying his confidence. "Bound by your own words and conditions that you set in place seven years ago. I'd be bound to your court, caught betwixt and between unless one from my own family could pass your tests and free me. We've passed your test, met your conditions. Does your word hold?"

The standards flapped in a sudden gust of wind, banners whisked here and there by a whirlwind. Then Aelwa, Queen of the Bog, intoned a voice like a death knell, "My word holds. But if I had known what you did before this night, Tam Lane, I would have turned you into a tree, plucked out your heart, or ripped out both your eyes so you could never again find your way by water."

With this last bitter pronouncement, the procession of the Dead Court and its kelpies and riders melted into the river, the wisps extinguished, leaving them in the night, alone.

Tam leaned his head and kissed Janet. "Thank you," he whispered. "Did I hurt you?"

Janet stroked his beard and shook her head. The scratches and scores were worth it.

"I hurt *myself*, when the illusion took my voice and said I didn't want you," he admitted, voice rough. "I'll always want you, Jan."

"I know, Tam." She smiled, pressed a kiss to his lips and took his hand again. "Let's go home."

Also by Claire Trella Hill

About the Author

Claire Trella Hill will read anything, but fantasy romance and gothic fiction are her favorites. Born and raised in Houston, Texas, she still lives there because she is impervious to 100 degree weather. She also has a bad habit of making her characters in the Sims and continuing their stories. When Claire isn't writing, she can be found with her nose glued to her library app, assisting with the last tricky pieces of a puzzle, swilling Dr. Pepper, collecting vintage romance covers, or cuddling with her cat.

You can connect with her on social media or sign up for her newsletter on her website ClaireTrellaHill.com.